resist

Donna,
Can you resist
Devlin Pierce?
xoxo
Lilly Avalon

LILLY AVALON

Cover design by Marie Landry, www.sweetmarie-83.blogspot.ca/
Edited by Stephanie Parent, www.stephanieparent.blogspot.com/
Formatting by Champagne Formats, www.ChampagneFormats.com

resist

Allegra Maxwell is sick of the monotony of life. It's all work and no play, and right now she wants to play. She shows up at her company's yearly meeting with one goal in mind: have a one-night stand with a stranger. What she doesn't count on is Devlin Pierce walking through the door.

When Allegra first met Devlin, she knew he would be nothing but trouble. After he proved her theory true last year, she made a vow to avoid him at all costs. He's the last person she wants to see, and he knows it. He refuses to leave her alone though. As much as she tries to fight it, the pull he has on her is undeniable. Her ability to resist him proves impossible when Devlin makes her an offer she can't refuse.

One night. That's all he asks. That's all she wants. Or is it?

also by

LILLY AVALON

Here All Along
More Than Words
Longing
Unexpected

dedication

To the real embodiment of the fictional Devlin Pierce,
wherever he is. May we meet somewhere other than just
my dreams someday, okay?

chapter one

This is a mistake.

Not pairing the silver stilettos with my brand new blue dress—no, that was genius. The mistake is coming here tonight when I should have stayed in my hotel room. It's not like I couldn't come up with a believable excuse. I'm relatively good under pressure. Not to mention the fact that lounging in nothing but a robe and watching from my window as the sun sets behind the Manhattan skyline sounded exceptionally better.

Why am I here, then? I'm on a mission.

The lobby in the Quartz Hotel is exquisite. Red velvet-cushioned chairs and golden framed early 1900s-style artwork line the walls. You feel like you've traveled back in time, expecting to find a mink stole draped over your shoulder when you peer into one of the vintage mirrors. This whole place is much fancier than I usually am. Tonight, however...

Stepping off the elevator into the lobby should bring a smile to my face. Instead, I'm sighing as the doors close behind me and the nerves creep in. There's still time to push the button and get the hell out of here.

"Allegra!"

Well, there goes *that* option.

When I turn, an older gentleman is walking in my direction. "Mr. Morris!" I say as I shake his hand, flashing him a huge grin. "It's so great to see you again." Mr. Morris, or Walter as his close friends know him, is the founder of the company I work for, Morris Enterprises. His goal upon finishing college was to start his own business. After a few failed ventures with fellow businessmen, he finally started Morris Enterprises. We dabble in various types of online businesses, including a website that sells quality office supplies. Twenty years later, the company is still running strong, largely thanks to his determination.

When Mr. Morris smiles, his forehead wrinkles, giving away his age. "Oh, Allegra Maxwell, it's always a pleasure to see you. How's Jack been treating you?"

"Very well."

"Wonderful. You look great, by the way." He gestures to my dress.

I glance down, and then back up at him. "Oh, thank

you. So do you. So spiffy." I touch his arm lightly. "Tell me, how's your wife? Is she here? I'd love to say hello."

He shakes his head. "Unfortunately, Beverly had to stay home tonight. She's been feeling a little under the weather lately with the temperature changes."

Lucky bitch, I think. I give him a disappointed frown. "Oh, that's too bad. Please send her my love."

"I will definitely do that, Allegra. You enjoy yourself tonight and try not to get into too much trouble." He gives me a wink as he shakes my hand one more time before he walks away.

Now that Mr. Morris has seen me, there's no escaping. *Get ready for two hours of forced smiles and sucking up to bosses and executives.* The annual company dinner may have the most delectable dishes and desserts, but it's boring as hell. The only thing that saves it is the men who show up. At least half of them are good-looking, handsome, and, dare I say it, sexy. Which brings me back to my mission and why I chose tonight to carry it out.

When I hit my mid-twenties last month, it felt like hitting rock bottom. I spent four years climbing to the top of this company straight out of college. I may have achieved success and a strong foundation for the future complete with a full benefits package, but there's not much to show for it, aside from a padded bank account. Yet, after all that overtime, what's the point of money when you have nobody to spend time with?

It's been years since I had a boyfriend. In fact, my last serious boyfriend was in college, and that's just depressing. I want nothing more than to settle down and have a steady relationship again. However, my job makes that nearly impossible, and the last time I *had* a relationship… Let's just say it didn't go as expected. Since I can't get serious with anyone, I've settled on the next best thing: a one-night stand with a complete stranger.

Don't get me wrong, I would love to find "The One". Every girl wants to find him. Since I haven't found any suitable contenders for the position, I might as well have some fun while I'm still young. And let's face it, I have needs—needs that haven't been taken care of in a year.

A whole year.

Screw finding The One. I just need *one* night. That's all I ask, at least for now. A palate cleanser, if you will. I need to feel that desire—the *longing*—that comes with a roll in the hay. I haven't felt it in a while, and I'm overdue for it. Long overdue. A girl can only take care of herself for so long until she needs someone who has the equipment for the job.

Before I have to go suffer through the dinner, I find a spot off to the side but in full view of anyone walking into our private dining room. I take my phone discreetly out of my clutch and speed-dial my best friend, Sonya. The first thing she says is, "Why are you calling me? Aren't you on a mission?"

"That's why I called. I need moral support."

"There's nothing moral about what you're about to do."

I accidentally let out half a snort, then bite my lip to keep from cracking up entirely. "Stop it, Miss Wallace. Don't make me laugh. If Jack catches me on the phone, I have to look like I'm on an important call."

"Yeah, I don't think our boss would be too pleased to know you're scouting for bedroom talent. Speaking of which, how are the prospects?"

"Haven't really spotted many yet. I just got down here, though." A couple younger men walk out of the elevator toward the dining room. "There we go."

"Score."

They're both probably in their early twenties. The taller of the two has caramel-blond wavy hair, the kind long enough to run your fingers through. The other has darker, shorter hair, and a chiseled jaw. They glance in my direction and I give them a flirtatious smile. I can tell by the look in their eyes that I've already hooked them. I'm extremely thankful for this dress. It has the perfect balance of elegant and sexy with enough professionalism to get away with it. I'm also appreciative of the subtle highlights I had my colorist put in my hair, which I spent the last hour curling in between putting on my makeup. "Just a matter of time before I reel one in."

"Ew." She's pretending to be disgusted, but I know better. Sonya and I may not go way back, but we've bonded since I started working at Morris Enterprises. We're incapable of hiding what we really think from each other.

I sigh. "I know what you're going to say." Ever since she got engaged, Sonya's been having a rough time trying to fulfill the wing-woman role in our friendship. It's not that she doesn't care, she's just been too focused on the wedding and the idea of finally being married. But she *is* interested in helping me find happiness. She wishes it were with someone special instead of this convoluted plan, though.

"I know you know, that's why I'm not going to say anything."

"Thank you. But I still hate you right about now."

"Why? Because I'm happy with Rodney?"

"Yes."

"That's no reason to hate someone." She sighs, and I can picture her rolling her eyes. "Look, just have one final fling tonight so that you can come home happy. Then we'll start our search for The One for you."

I want to be hopeful of the elusive One but I can't stop being cynical. "Good luck finding a guy that isn't a complete waste of a man."

"I don't even know how to respond to that."

Another younger man comes out of the elevator and stops to talk to Mr. Morris. "Well, hello there."

"Ooh, another one? What does he look like?"

"Something tall, dark, and handsome." I press my lips together to hold back the laugh.

"Something? Don't you mean someone?"

"Probably."

"In all seriousness, though…what does he look like? Face, eyes…"

"Well, unfortunately I can't get a good look at him."

"Why not?"

"He's facing the other way." Squinting my eyes, I try to see if I can make out the details of the handsome something. He's wearing a very expensive suit by the looks of it, navy pinstripe over white button down. He obviously works out based on how perfectly tailored it is. I mean, that ass… Yowza. That's all I can see from this angle though. *Come on, show me your face. I need something to boost my spirits.*

He finally finishes his conversation with Mr. Morris, and starts walking toward the dining hall. After a few steps, the light hits his face just right so I can make out his features. He seems familiar, very familiar. That's when I gasp. I recognize the well-defined face. The dark brown hair. The smoldering dark emerald eyes.

"Anything?" Sonya says.

"Holy shit," I breathe, nearly dropping my phone. This can't be happening.

"That good, huh?"

I can barely speak, but not for the reason she's thinking. I'm flabbergasted. Floored, even. He looks familiar because I *have* seen him before—right at this very place—almost exactly a year ago. My heart races and breaks all at once when the memory returns. I thought I had buried it back then.

"Allegra? Are you still there?"

Somehow, I discover my voice again. "I'm gonna have to call you back." I hang up on her before she can respond. I'm not sure what to do with myself. I'm not sure of anything at this moment.

Because the man who stepped off that elevator is Devlin Pierce, and his eyes have landed on mine.

chapter two

"**Y**ou've got to be kidding me," I say under my breath.

If it had been a year ago that I was standing here, it would be impossible not to admit my interest. Not just impossible—*absolutely* inconceivable. He still looks irresistibly handsome with those full lips and the allure in his eyes. Also, the way he carries himself, his commanding presence, hasn't changed. The only thing that's different is that he's clean-shaven, unlike that hard-to-keep-your-fingers-off stubble from last year.

But it isn't last year.

How could I forget that Devlin Pierce would be here? Have I gone temporarily insane to the point where I can't remember such important details? He *is* Jack's nephew, for crying out loud. Of course he would be here again. And, *of course*, he would be heading right for me.

He approaches me, sizing me up from head to toe. I leave my expression blank, not because I want to keep my thoughts as a mystery, but because I have no idea where my mind is. All I know is that I'm in the same building as him and he's about to get under my skin, and not in the good way.

He reaches me quickly, barely allowing me a moment of recovery from my panic. There's a smug joy in his eyes as they connect with mine. "Ah Allegra, we meet again at last."

His voice is like fire, coursing through me, stirring up the desire I initially felt for him. The desire quickly fades into a painful burn and I flinch inwardly. Looking around, I furrow my brows. "Wait a second. Where am I? Because I could've sworn the last time I saw you, I told you to go to hell."

He frowns. "Come on, Allegra. You can't still be mad at me." I'd believe he is truly upset if it weren't for the puppy dog eyes he's giving me.

"You expect me to just let it go like *that*?" I snap my fingers.

He shakes his head. "That's not it at all. It's been a year and you never even gave me a chance to explain myself." He takes one step closer to me, his eyes pleading.

He wants to talk, but I'm not in the mood. I hold up a hand. "I don't want to hear your 'explanation,' Devlin."

He pushes down my hand, reaching out to take a lock of my hair between his fingers. "I really wish you would," he murmurs.

The scent of his cologne begins to seep in, dulling the rest of my senses. You know, the kind of cologne the government should make illegal because it short-circuits your brain. It's like a great panty dropper, overpowering your sense of decency. That, along with the intimacy of his move, stirs up those long lost feelings of the brief moment we shared last year. It takes me a few seconds to register what he's doing. I smack his hand away with my arm. "Don't hold your breath."

He sighs heavily as he steps back. "Look, I have no expectations. It would just be nice to have some level of respect as colleagues. Or, at the very least, you could be cordial."

I cross my arms over my chest. "This *is* me being cordial." If only he knew how nice I'm being at this moment.

He seems to realize this, but it doesn't appear to faze him. He cocks his head, saying, "I doubt that." He looks toward the dining room. "Have you seen Jack?" he asks, apparently giving up on changing my mind.

"No, I haven't." I allow myself to breathe in his heavenly scent as casually as I can without his notice. It really irks me how much I love the way he smells.

"Well, I suppose I ought to find him. It really is nice to see you again, Allegra." He nods to me, and then walks away.

"I wish I could say the same," I call after him. He glances back at me, smiling. He's *smiling* at my remark. What the hell is his problem?

According to the old-fashioned clock on the wall next to me, dinner will be starting in only a few minutes. I knew this was a bad idea. I wish I had stayed in my hotel room after all. I want nothing more than to get out of here, but several people have already seen me. I can't leave now; I need to suck it up and stay for dinner. It's possible Devlin may have ruined the chances of me taking some random hottie to bed, so I deserve a free meal out of the night at least.

I sigh loudly. This dinner better not last too long.

After about a minute of deep breathing, I reluctantly saunter toward the dining hall, head held high. It doesn't take long for Jack to spot me. His shoulders relax and he hurries over. "There you are," he says as he locks my elbow with his. "I was beginning to worry."

I touch a hand to my heart. "Worry about me? I wouldn't miss this for the world."

He gives me a serious look. "You better not. Mr. Morris likes you and our branch could do well to expand a little bit."

I ask, "He does?" Jack nods. Huh. Guess all that sucking up pays off after all.

He drags me over to our table. I can already smell the aroma of our upcoming dishes for the night. They probably hired the same catering company as last year. *Maybe this won't be so bad,* I think. *Good meal, fine wine, delectable dessert…* That's when Devlin comes over to my table and that theory is dashed to pieces. Why would I think I could escape Devlin when I'm sitting with Jack?

Jack gestures toward Devlin and says to me, "You remember my nephew, don't you, Allegra?"

Do I remember him? Yes, I do. Do I *want* to remember him? That's another story. I give Devlin a sweet smile and shake his hand. "Of course I remember. How could I *ever* forget that night?"

Devlin raises an eyebrow, but smiles back. "I don't think I could forget it either. Your hair looks very lovely tonight, Allegra." The smug look reappears as he holds out my chair for me.

An overwhelming urge to smack him comes over me, but I keep my cool as I sit down. "Thank you, Devlin. You're such a gentleman." Thankfully, my sarcasm doesn't come through too much in my voice.

"You have no idea," he says as he takes a seat across the table from me. He tilts his head, and it feels like he's challenging me. To what, I'm not sure. I do know one thing, though.

This is going to be a long night.

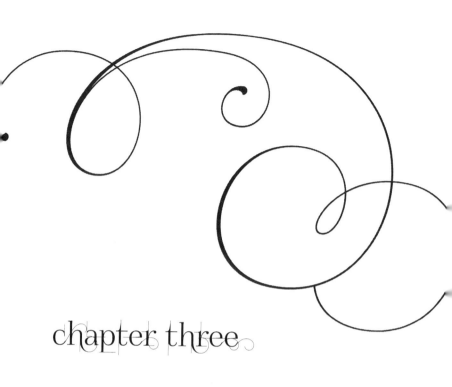

chapter three

Dinner lasts about an hour with all the courses—starting with an almond chicken salad, then fettuccine Alfredo, ending with a silky chocolate truffle cheesecake. The cheesecake is to die for. Unfortunately, I'm unable to enjoy it thanks to Devlin. He isn't directly bothering me; he's been talking to Jack and the other associates at our table. It's just his presence that annoys me.

Jack is deep in conversation with Miles, the boss at Devlin's branch in Florida. They're discussing the new line of personalized pens we've made available recently. I let out a quiet sigh of boredom and go back to my dessert.

While I'm cutting a piece of the cheesecake with my fork, I catch Devlin watching me. Not just watching me, he's staring me down. I blink rapidly as heat washes over me.

Why is he looking at me like that? It's causing sensations in my lady parts that I forgot were even possible. He winks and somehow I know that he knows this. Bastard. I give him a slight head shake and lift my fork to my mouth, thinking he'll look away.

He doesn't.

Fine. Two can play at this game. I match his gaze as I place the cheesecake in my mouth, slowly pulling the fork out. I lick my lips seductively, never looking away. He stiffens in his seat, leaning forward slightly. I toss him a quick wink and go for the last bite. Taking my time, I slip the silky dessert between my open lips. After I use my forefinger to wipe my mouth clean, I place it in my mouth, licking the remainder of the chocolate off. At this point, his formerly open hand has turned into a fist. I'm getting to him. This makes me smile in victory.

The victory is short-lived because his eyes are still on me, remaining there as if they can't look away. Somehow, neither can I. Our eyes stay locked for the longest time, refusing to veer away. Finally, I break the spell, turning my head to the side, letting go of the breath I was holding. What is happening to me? Why am I taunting him with sexual innuendo? And why is this whole thing turning me on?

Now that I'm finished with my dessert, I have no reason to stay at the table. Touching my napkin to my mouth, I say, "Excuse me a moment." Jack gives me a nod, allowing me to leave. I stand and walk off, not even giving Devlin another glance. I'm afraid to look at him with the power he seems to have over my body.

I go back to my vantage point from earlier and call Sonya back. She answers on the first ring. "What the hell happened? Why did you hang up on me?"

"Devlin Pierce is here!" I say through clenched teeth.

"What are you talking about?"

"Remember that guy from last year—"

"The one you caught kissing the blonde bombshell with the big boobs?"

"Wow, that's a lot of B words," I mumble as I try to block the visual that comes with her words. "Yes, that's the guy."

"Holy shit. What are you going to do?"

"I don't know. Get out of here before he starts to break down my defenses."

"Oh man." She whistles. "He's pulling you in again."

My jaw drops. "What? He is not."

"He is. You're obviously attracted to him still. I already know he's attracted to you."

"No, he isn't." The thing is, I know she's right based on the way he watched me just a couple of minutes ago. What I did probably caused him to get a hard on. The thought of being able to elicit that kind of response from a man gives me a thrill. *Damn my body! Stop trying to do the job of my brain and heart.*

"The guy *did* chase you down last year."

"To make excuses," I insist.

She audibly sighs over the phone. "I know you're going to hate me for this, but I think Devlin might very well be the best thing to do right now. Pun intended."

"Are you *kidding*? The bastard would enjoy it too much."

"From how you described him, so would you...So would I, engaged or not."

Shaking my head, I say, "You can have him."

"Please. I don't *really* want him. I'm quite satisfied with my prince."

"You know, I have half a mind to hop on a plane and teach you some manners."

A voice behind me says, "Leaving so soon?"

Spinning around, I find Devlin standing only a couple feet away. How long has he been there? What did he hear? My nostrils flare. "I'm not planning on staying long."

"Is that him?" Sonya asks.

"Yes."

Devlin asks, "Who are you talking to?"

"None of your business."

He snatches my phone from me and says to Sonya, "Miss Allegra is being evasive and she won't tell me your name...Ah, Sonya. Perhaps you could help me out by explaining why she's in such a hurry to escape."

"Give me my phone back!" I reach to grab for my phone but he holds me at bay with a hand on my shoulder. I flinch at his touch and step away.

"Uh-huh," he says, raising his eyebrows at me. "I see."

"What do you see?" I ask him.

"Thank you, Sonya, you've been very helpful."

Helpful? He holds out my phone and I grab it from him angrily. I put the phone back up to my ear, not taking my eyes off Devlin. "What did you say to him?"

"Nothing!" she says.

"Liar," I say. Devlin continues to stand in front of me, a classic devilish look across his face. I sigh. "I need to go, Sonya."

"Live out the fantasy for me, please. I live vicariously through you."

"Hanging up now." I end the call, toss my phone back in my clutch, and glare at Devlin.

He tilts his head and frowns. "That was rude of you."

"Me? What about you?"

"I apologize for taking your phone, but I needed an answer."

The audacity of this man! "What did she tell you?"

He smirks. "Exactly what I expected."

I let out a groan of exasperation. "Excuse me." I turn on my heel to the elevator.

"We're not done yet, Allegra," Devlin calls after me.

"Oh yeah, why's that?" I ask as I push the button to go up.

He stands in front of me, blocking the elevator. "Jack sent me out here to make sure you were okay."

Stepping closer to him, I press a finger to his chest. "You can tell him I was feeling out of it and had to go back to my room." I lift my hand away only to have him catch it in his. Holding my hand over his heart, his fingers curl around mine. My palm soaks in the heat of his chest through his clothes. A powerful sensation spreads down to my toes, and my heart skips a beat, the intoxication of his scent holding me there.

"Is that the truth?" he asks, his eyes searching mine. "Or is it something else?"

I stare into the deep pools of his eyes. There's a shift in the atmosphere. I'm barely aware of him moving in closer, leaning toward me, toward my lips. My eyes are closing of their own initiative, completely ignoring the warning siren blaring in my skull. It's not loud enough. I'm no longer listening. It isn't until the elevator chimes that I realize what is happening. I jerk away from him, yanking my hand from his chest. The spell is broken and I'm not going to let him drown me in it again.

I give him a slight shove to push him out of my way, and rush into the empty elevator. I push the button for my floor and look at him. He blinks a few times as if he's trying to register what just happened. "I'll never tell," I say as the doors close between us.

chapter four

Once I reach my floor, I take a brief moment to catch my breath from what just occurred between us. It was potent, almost tangible. A shiver runs through me, but I shake it off.

I walk over to a different elevator that isn't near the dining hall and go back downstairs to the hotel lounge. It looks a lot like the rest of the hotel, only slightly less of a throwback, and different color scheme. I sit on a dark blue cushioned barstool that matches my dress and order a Long Island. As I wait for my drink, I glance around and notice the music I'm hearing isn't from speakers but from an actual band of musicians on a stage. I close my eyes to listen closely to see if I can remember what it is. It's instrumental and familiar, but I can't quite place my finger on it.

resist

Once I get my drink and take a few sips, I allow myself to relax for the first time this evening. I peruse the prospects in the bar, finding a couple possibilities. Maybe tonight isn't over for the mission after all. I almost went back to my hotel room alone, no thanks to that troublesome bastard.

Ever since I started with the company, Jack wanted to introduce Devlin to me. Unfortunately, Devlin kept missing out on the annual meetings until last year. Right before the dinner, we had an extensive staring contest from across the room. The electricity from that stare alone could have powered the hotel for the rest of the night. Before Jack could introduce us, Devlin waltzed over to introduce himself to me, neither of us even knowing who the other was. We didn't say much—it amounted to mostly business and small talk. But then, right before he walked away, he leaned in close and whispered, "Allegra, I would very much like to do more than just talk about work with you."

I shivered at his words. I didn't need Taylor Swift to tell me he was trouble; his gaze alone told me that. Still, I said to him, "I would love that." We spent the majority of the evening exchanging glances from across the table, glances that sent shivers through me and created dampness in my panties. It wasn't long after that he—

I don't want to think about it. It's in the past. Devlin is in the past. How dare he mess with my head? He lied to me before, so I can't tell what is really going on in that big head of his. As much as I force myself to be mad at him, I can't stop fantasizing about him. About his body on top of mine, his lips caressing my…

No. I need to just stop thinking about him and relax. Put the earlier part of this night behind me and enjoy myself. Live in the present. Find someone to get my mind off my life. I can think about the future tomorrow.

I make eye contact with a somewhat cute guy across the room and lift up my chest, winking. He smirks, standing up with his drink and walking this way. Well, at least this night won't be a total loss. I face the bar again and take a deep breath. Here we go.

"You do realize they're serving liquor at the bar in the dining hall, and on the company's dime no less."

I snap my head to the right and find Devlin standing there. "What the hell are you doing here?"

He sits down casually on the stool next to me. "I'm just here for a drink. Oh, and to talk about that almost kiss in front of the elevator."

I twitch almost imperceptibly. The guy from across the room is already retreating now that Devlin has effectively claimed me by stealing the stool next to mine. I might as well count on a night alone at this point. "I have no idea what you're talking about." I return to my drink.

"Cut the bullshit."

I jerk my head toward him. "It's no bullshit. We didn't kiss."

"I didn't say that we did, I said we *almost* did. After

that *and* the stunt you pulled at dinner, you expect to leave without me seeking you out?"

"Yes," I grumble, turning back to the bar.

"Well, you thought wrong." He leans over, his jacket brushing against my bare arm. "For someone who allegedly has no interest in me, you sure as hell enjoy teasing me. Why?"

"Because I'm a shameless flirt?"

"I don't think that's it."

"Cocktease?"

"You're too nice to be a cocktease."

I turn to him, my eyes flashing. "Then what do you think it is?"

He moves in closer, enough that the tingly feeling you experience right before a kiss looms inside my stomach again. He stops about three inches from my face. He's so close I can make out flecks of blue in between the emerald of his irises. "You're attracted to me."

I can't move. I can't even turn my head away. "That's not it."

"You *were* attracted to me before," he says in a low voice, his eyes darkening. "You can't deny it."

"Yes, I was," I concede. "Doesn't mean I still am."

"I don't believe you."

"A lot can change in a year, you know."

"A lot can stay the same, too." He pulls away finally, and I feel a tug in my heart that's disappointed at the loss.

Damn it, now my heart's trying to ruin me.

"So, why are you down here?" he asks. "You're a smart girl. I don't know why you would let an opportunity for free booze go to waste."

I close my eyes. Why won't he just go away? It's as if he's intentionally poking me until I wake up to tear him a new one. "Well, up until a minute ago, you weren't in the lounge, so…"

He lets out a chuckle. "Ah, I see."

"Good. Now do me a favor: make like a tree and leave."

"You'd like that, wouldn't you?"

"That's why I suggested it."

In my peripheral vision, I sense him coming near again. "You claim that you want me to leave, but I have a feeling you don't want me to."

I angle my head in his direction. "What makes you think that?"

"I saw the way you were looking at me earlier…and despite the anger in those eyes right now, I can feel the lust radiating off your skin." He lifts a finger to my lips to keep me from responding. "You can deny it all you want to me, but you need to stop lying to yourself."

He pulls his finger away and I say flatly, "Attraction means nothing if I can't trust a man."

He leans back. "You can trust me, Allegra. The only reason you don't is because you won't give me the chance to explain what happened."

"But—"

"Stop." He holds up a hand to keep me from cutting him off again. "Please afford me the opportunity to tell you the truth."

He's pleading with me and I can't imagine why. Unless what I thought I saw wasn't really what I saw. However…I did see the kiss with my own eyes. Would it really hurt for me to let him explain? Maybe he'll leave me alone if I do. "Fine. Tell me."

He lets out a sigh of relief. "Last year, my branch in Florida invited one of the interns to come with us. Her name is Jenna. She had a thing for me since her first day. I needed to tread lightly; I didn't want her to think I was interested, but I didn't want her to think I was a jerk either. She misread my signals of just being nice as something more. She was the one that cornered *me* to steal a kiss." He rubs the back of his neck and looks away. "As soon as I saw you, my heart sank. I knew you would misunderstand what you saw."

My hand goes to my mouth. "That's why you chased after me."

He looks back up at me and nods. "I don't cheat—never have, never will. It was tearing me up inside that you probably thought that. When you brushed me off, I was crushed." He rubs his cheek. "Sometimes I still feel the sting from where you slapped me."

A powerful urge to kiss that cheek overcomes me, but I hold back. "I'm sorry, Devlin. I shouldn't have assumed the worst."

"You probably had your reasons."

"Maybe." He's right; I did. But that part of my life is behind me, too.

"I'm aware of my reputation as a womanizer. That claim is founded on baseless evidence, yet it still seems to follow me wherever I go. The worst of it is that I had turned over a new leaf right before I met you." He shakes his head, and then our eyes meet. "Allegra?"

"Yes?"

"Can we call a truce?"

He sincerely wants to make things right with me, and that I can admire. I still don't know if I can trust him, but it's not because of what I thought happened. It's because I don't really know him yet. Despite that, I have this feeling inside telling me that I should give him a chance. Like he said earlier, we can at least be cordial with one another. Colleagues. Acquaintances. Maybe even friends eventually.

I answer, "No."

He frowns. "Why not?"

"Because you only call a truce when there's something to fight about. I have nothing against you." I give him a warm smile. "The real question is can you forgive me for being a bitch?"

He shakes his head. "No. That would require you to be one in the first place."

We laugh together. It feels nice to leave the animosity

behind us. "Stay and have a drink with me," I tell him.

"That's what I was planning on doing."

chapter five

After Devlin orders our drinks, he turns to me and says, "So, now that we're friends—"

"I never said we were friends."

"—we can be upfront with each other, right?"

I'm giving him the benefit of the doubt that he's telling me the truth about last year. I only saw the kiss from a distance, so I couldn't see the look on his face to know whether she caught him off guard or what. He seems sincere, but it doesn't change the fact that I don't know him. "I can be honest, but I don't open up to everybody."

"Fair enough." The bartender places our drinks in front of us, and Devlin hands him some cash. After he walks away, Devlin takes a swig of his scotch. He looks at me closely and, leaning forward slightly, says, "You look absolutely stunning tonight."

I roll my eyes, but flush at his words. "Stop," I tell him, even though I want him to continue with the flattery.

"There's something about it, though."

"What about it?" I sip at my drink, not wanting to be too liquored up while I'm near Devlin. There's no telling when my brain will choose to give up control to my body. Better not take away the last shred of sanity holding me—and my legs—together.

He sets his drink down, but swirls it around. "The way you're dressed to the nines tonight—it's not because you needed to. It's because you *wanted* to." He pauses to peek up at me. "Almost like you're on a mission."

Holy hell! My eyes widen and my fingers clench into a fist. "Sonya *did* tell you! I'm gonna kick her ass on Monday." I slam my fist on the bar. How dare she tell Devlin of all people about my mission? This quite possibly could have been the worst thing to happen tonight.

"I think I'd better get her number so I can warn her about these threats," he says with a chuckle. "But right now, I'd like to know more about this mission."

"What makes you think you can get me to talk about it?"

"Because you want to tell me."

"Why would I want to tell you?"

"I think you know why."

It's obvious that he wants me to let him in—not just

in, but all the way in. Why, however, I have no clue. None whatsoever. He barely knows me, and I barely know him. Aside from a couple brief conversations when we first met, the real him is still a just-cracked-opened book. Not that I wouldn't mind reading more, I just don't know how I'll feel about what I'm going to find.

He says, "You know, Allegra, you need to stop assuming the worst about guys based on what you've seen in movies. Not all of us are assholes. Some are just curious."

Tilting my head, I really look at him and say the first thing that comes to mind. "Are you one of those guys who enjoys dominating a woman?"

He stops swirling his drink and glances at me. "Is that what you want?"

"No. It's just…the way you carry yourself sometimes, makes me wonder."

"Is that so?" he asks, slowly sitting up straighter.

I nod.

He raises an eyebrow, studying my face. Then he suddenly bursts out laughing. Devlin Pierce is laughing at me.

I place a hand on my hip. "What is so funny?"

"You. You're just an intense mess of crazy thoughts."

Glaring at him, I ask, "Is that an insult?"

He shakes his head and regains his composure. "Not at all. In fact, it's what I like about you: you're not afraid to just say something—*anything*—that comes to that pretty little mind of yours." He touches my forehead with his finger and

resist

smiles. "It's endearing."

I've never heard anyone call the way my mind works anything other than strange or crazy. This catches me off guard, but in a good way. "Most men find it intimidating."

"Intimidating?"

I nod and sigh. "Yeah, I draw their attention, but they change their mind when they hear what I have to say."

"I want to hear what you have to say," he says in a soft voice, his gaze focused entirely on me.

Something in me believes that he really does. For the first time in my life, a man actually wants to hear about the endless tumbling thoughts in my head. And for the first time in my life, I actually want to tell one.

"Fine," I say. "You want me to be honest? I'll be honest. I've reached the point in my life where it's either a breaking point or an epiphany. I have a love-hate relationship with relationships. I want one, but I hate the dickheads I keep finding. Because of this, I'm in a perpetual horny state. And a girl can only rely on her vibrator for so long. It's not the same as the real thing, not remotely. What's great about sex is human contact. The kisses and caresses. Not some rubber facsimile that vibrates and spins."

When Devlin chokes on his drink, it hits me that I just admitted to not only owning, but also *using* a vibrator. *Good going, Allegra.* So much for playing it cool and not trying to scare him. "It would be nice to have a random fuck to just… release the tension." I let out a breath. "So, there you have it."

At this point, I'm expecting him to run away like every other man. I avoid looking over to find the normally freaked-out face I'm used to seeing. After about fifteen seconds of silence, he says, "I do have to admit, you're correct. Real sex is better than sex with yourself."

I let out a light chuckle, relieved. "So, you understand the predicament."

"Yes and no. I understand needing to release the tension, but you don't strike me as the type to do this sort of thing."

"I'm not." My mission tonight completely goes against the regular me but that is the point. I need to let loose for once, just enough to break me out of my comfort zone.

"Then may I ask why? Because it almost seems like you're—"

"Contradicting myself? I know. I would love to find someone special instead of a stranger, believe me. Sonya's determined to assist me in finding 'The One' when I get home." Maybe Sonya will actually have luck finding a decent guy for me so that I can settle down, but I'm not going to hold my breath. "I know it sounds stupid…I want a relationship, but I want sex enough to forgo a relationship. Just for the one night, at least."

"It's not stupid. I can relate." He sets down his drink and leans against the bar, chin in his hand. "With all the overtime I work, I'm unable to give a woman what she really needs in a relationship. If someone is interested in going out on a date with me, I start by telling them straight up that I'm not the guy they're looking for. I rarely, if ever, have a girlfriend."

"You say you can relate, but I can tell you don't approve."

"It's not that I don't approve…my issue lies with it being random. Why a complete stranger?"

I close my eyes. I know where he's going with this. "I need to take what I can get because what I want is never there."

Leaning in close enough for me to feel his breath on my skin, he asks in a low voice, "What is it that you want?"

You, I think. But I'll never admit it out loud. It would be a mistake. The last thing I need in my life is another one of those mistakes, especially when I swore never to let that happen again. I look into his emerald eyes, trying to find some fault with him, but I'm not finding one. My resolve is crumbling with each and every second I'm spending next to him.

A strand of my hair falls in my face. Just as I'm reaching up to fix it, his hand is there, tucking it behind my ear. It's only a brushing of his fingers at the very edge of my ear, but it electrifies my body down to my toes.

"I think I know what you want," he says. "What you desire."

This is it. I know the next word coming from his lips when I ask my question. I attempt a steady voice that doesn't give anything away, but it's unstable. "What is it that I desire?"

"Me."

chapter six

He really does have a lot of nerve. My nostrils involuntarily flare at his bold assumption. I reply, "You think you can get me to go from zero to on my back in one minute with your sugared words?" Before he can respond, I continue. "Well, I'm not going for it. I get it, though—you're turned on. I mean who wouldn't be with my breasts practically spilling out." The amount of cleavage I'm displaying might actually be outlawed in some parts of the country.

He grows visibly tense at my comment. In a sharp tone, he retorts, "Oh, and you're *not* turned on? I saw the way you were looking at me earlier. I see the way you're looking at me now."

His ability to see right through me simultaneously

pisses me off and impresses me. "That's beside the point."

"So, you admit it?" he asks, eyebrows raised.

As if anyone could deny the sexual attraction between us. It is all I can do not to jump off my stool to straddle his lap, run my fingers through his thick hair, lifting my hips to rub our bodies together…

Am I fantasizing about dry humping Devlin in a bar? I think I am.

"If you already know the answer, why do you insist on asking?" I ask him.

"To confirm my suspicions."

"Consider them confirmed." I take a long sip from my drink and close my eyes. "It's all skin deep for us, though."

"You think my feelings are superficial because I'm physically attracted to you?"

"I think that's the definition of superficial."

"It's actually a bonus on the fact that you're a strong woman with more character and tenacity than any other woman I've been acquainted with."

"Tenacity?"

"Hell yeah. You drive me nuts."

My body goes still, then I turn to him. "I do?"

"Yes," he growls. He places a hand on my leg just above the hemline and I can barely breathe. "Just consider it. One night with someone who isn't a complete stranger."

With his hand there, I can hardly concentrate on every single reason why I shouldn't. "But you don't even know me."

"Who's fault is that?" He smirks. "I know enough about you to know that I *want* to know more." He squeezes my leg gently.

"How much more?"

"Everything."

It feels like he's proposing two different options at the same time. One that lasts briefly and one that could last forever. "Why would you offer me *one* night, then?"

He shrugs. "Because that's what you're looking for."

"What about you?"

"Like I said, I'm not looking for a serious relationship, not looking to disappoint a girlfriend or wife because my career is my primary focus. I may not be ready to settle down, but I don't lie about my intentions. I'm honest about them. I won't make a promise I can't deliver on. Marriage is not on my immediate agenda."

"But I am?"

"You're the one who's asking for one night. I'm just offering myself as an alternative to a random guy. It would be safer than a complete stranger."

I can't deny that he's absolutely right, but I can't help but be worried. "And after?"

"We're adults. You have no expectations for a relationship and neither do I. I'm sure we could act like professionals after if we meet at functions like this." He pauses and raises an eyebrow. "Or just fool around."

I roll my eyes. "How do I even know whether you're being honest or telling me what I want to hear?"

"It doesn't matter how I answer the question because you won't believe me."

"Touché." I start laughing, and then shake my head. "Can you blame me?"

"No, but someday you're gonna have to discern it yourself."

"How?"

"Body language. Eye contact. It's a skill you pick up over time. Or after years of playing poker."

"Maybe I should play poker."

"Strip poker?" One of his eyebrows quirks up and a hint of a smirk shows up at the edge of his lips.

"Don't push your luck."

"Then stop attempting to change the subject."

"I wasn't trying to." Maybe I was, a little bit. My mind is spinning with his words, with this idea. I press my lips together as my eyes flick down to his hand still on my leg.

"You haven't asked me to let go."

I peek up at him. "No, I haven't."

"You also haven't said anything in response to my proposal."

"I'm not sure what to say."

"That's because you're afraid of seeing how love should be."

I give him a dubious look. "Are you saying you love

me?"

"No. Wouldn't that be too improbable?"

"Very. So, you're being facetious?"

"Hardly. I'm making a point."

"Which is…?" I raise an eyebrow at him.

"Love isn't overnight, at least not for most people. But how about in the future?" Even though I say nothing in response, he already knows the words on the tip of my tongue. "I understand your distrust, Allegra, but you *do* believe that love exists, right?"

I nod. "Of course."

"Just not for you?"

I turn my head away to avoid his piercing gaze. Now his ability to read me is disconcerting. That, and strangely admirable. I shake my head at the fact that I could ever admire Devlin.

His fingers graze my chin, carefully turning my face back to his. "What is it, Allegra?"

In a voice barely above a whisper, I say, "I couldn't possibly imagine being loved like women are in the movies."

He frowns at this. "That's no way to live your life."

"How else *can* I when all I've suffered is heartbreak while all my peers marry and have children? I feel like I'm one of the spinsters in a Jane Austen novel."

"You're only twenty-five, for God's sake."

"Exactly." Halfway through my twenties with no prospects in life. No suitors, no love, no happiness.

"You're still young. You may be sexy as hell but you're not just some pretty face. You're smart, sophisticated, honest, and incredibly funny. Most guys are terrified of a woman who can give them a run for their money. They want a woman they can easily manipulate, someone who's just arm candy. Not me."

"What do you want?"

He takes my hand in his. "The whole package. Beauty is only skin deep. I want a woman with everything, one who fulfills my desires physically and emotionally." He's playing with my fingers, weaving his around mine, then letting go only to do it again. He makes eye contact and brings my hand up to his lips. He presses a warm kiss on top of my hand, and then turns it over to place one on my palm.

When he lets go of my hand, I almost reach to grab his again. I finally breathe and it comes out a little shaky. Silently, I curse myself for feeling something. He's getting to me.

Oh, boy, is he getting to me.

"So, what am I?" I ask.

"You're everything a man with any sense would want."

Closing my eyes, I shake my head slightly. "You're just saying that."

"No, I'm not. I don't just go up to every woman and say these things to them."

"No, you just do that with me." He raises an eyebrow and the truth of what I just stated hits me. "Oh."

"One night," he says. "You're looking for a man to give

you one night of passion. It shouldn't be just any man. It should be with me."

"You?"

"Yes, me. With me it wouldn't be random."

"What will it be then?"

"It'll be more."

It'll be more. It'll be more meaningful—not just a random fuck with some guy I don't give a damn about. It'll be with this guy—the one whose words send a rush of sensations throughout my entire body. It'll be a night I'll always remember until I become an old woman sitting in a rocking chair on a countryside porch. It's also a dangerous notion, one that could land my heart in a prison of its own making. He's overriding my common sense, and I'm letting him do it.

He raises an eyebrow slowly. "You've thought about it. I can tell because you're already blushing."

I turn away, cursing my face for telling the truth. "Stop."

"No." He places the palm of his hand on my cheek, turning my face back to his, and keeps it there. "I'm not going to beg; I'm just offering the option. You're completely free to say no. We can do whatever you want tonight, Allegra. Imagine your wildest fantasy brought to life. I'm game for anything."

"Anything? Really?" I say breathlessly.

"I'd be a willing participant in *any* of your fantasies."

I hold back a shudder at the thought of him being the

man in one of my many fantasies. "And…hypothetically, of course…if we do this, then what? We just wake up the next morning and walk away?"

"If that's what you want." He takes his hand away and holds up a finger. "I only ask for one thing."

A creeping anticipation builds in my stomach. "What's that?"

"I want one kiss."

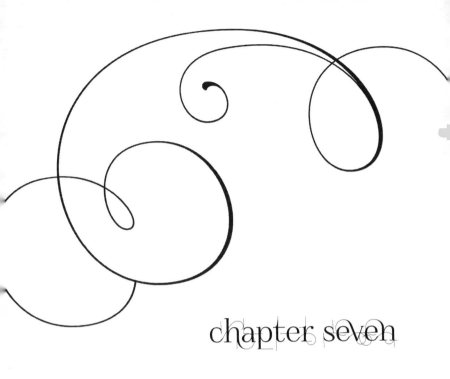

chapter seven

A kiss? He could ask me for anything, and that is what he requests. "You want to kiss me?"

There's a blaze to his eyes as he stares at me. "I want to do more than kiss you, but I'm asking for just one kiss. Besides…" He touches a finger to my bottom lip. "We probably owe one to the universe for chickening out earlier."

"Why only one?"

"Because that's all it would take to convince you that one night would be worth it."

Of course. He thinks he has a magic kiss that can bring me to life. Well, I'm not Sleeping Beauty, and this isn't a fairy tale. No fairy tales I've heard of include sex; at least, none I heard when I was a kid.

He can sense my hesitation. "Don't worry. I won't kiss

you the second you say yes. I have to hold the suspense."

I think about it. What he's offering is actually brilliant. He's giving me the option to sleep with him, not expecting anything. So, what harm could one kiss do? "Fine, *one* kiss," I say, holding up one finger to emphasize.

He flashes a dazzling smile, and I suddenly feel like a fly heading straight for a spider's web. One kiss may seem innocent enough, but I'm beginning to wonder how smart my decision is. If his kiss does entice me—if I do give in and we sleep together—what will that mean? Am I the kind of woman who can walk away from a night of passion with no regrets and never look back?

He says pointedly, "You look like you already regret this."

"I don't."

"Trust me, you won't."

There's something about that gleam in his eyes that proves I can trust him. Whether I can trust him on anything else, that's another story. Honestly, I want to trust him beyond a solitary kiss. But, who's to say whether he's for real or just a product of my own imagination? Part of me hopes that he's for real, but the other part doesn't want him to be. because if he is then that makes *this* real. I may have wanted it last year when I met him, but I'm a different person now, and so is he. He revealed what really happened last year and I believe him. Then why don't I trust him? Maybe it has less to do with him and more to do with me.

resist

Devlin breaks me out of my reverie. "Let's have some fun tonight."

My head snaps in his direction, my eyes narrowing.

"Not that kind of fun. I realize it's hard to get your mind out of the gutter with me around, but come on. I've gotta hand it to you, though, because it would be fucking awesome. What I mean is, just fun. Enjoy ourselves."

"How do we do that?"

"What kind of music do you like?"

I make a face at him. "Is this the 'getting to know you' portion of the evening?"

"If I don't ask the important questions, no one will. So?"

"I listen to a lot of stuff."

His gaze travels from me to the band in the opposite corner of the room then back to me again. "Stuff like this?" He gestures toward the band.

"Sometimes." They've been playing a variety tonight from classical to smooth jazz. Something about it brings back nostalgic memories from childhood.

"Do you like to dance?"

"Yes," I say slowly.

"Because I like to dance."

I open my mouth to speak when he holds up a finger, gets up, and walks toward the band. What the hell is he doing? He gestures to the guitarist and whispers something. I attempt to resist the urge to stare at Devlin, yet my eyes can't look away. He's just as sexy as he was a year ago, if not more. The well-defined chin and jawline, the luscious lips, and the way he carries himself—that confidence that just bleeds through, forcing you to take notice. I'm curious what he's asking them to play, but I can't stop the drifting of my thoughts. Would one night be such a bad idea?

Devlin shakes hands with the guitarist and comes back to me. When he takes my hand in his, the band begins to play. I raise my eyebrows at him. "Salsa?"

"You know your Latin music?" He leads me across the room until we're in an open area near the band.

I shrug and let go of his hand. "Some."

"The real question is, can you dance?"

"You tell me." I place one hand around his shoulder and take his hand with the other. He places his hand on that sweet spot between my waist and bottom. It's in this moment, with our bodies this close, that I realize I'm a goner. Devlin knows what he's doing with the seductive music that requires such physical intimacy. It's going to take everything to hold myself together.

We take the first steps tentatively, but once he realizes I know what I'm doing, everything shifts between us. The dance is passionate. We move in tempo, our bodies entangled in an embrace while our legs guide us across the floor. I lose myself in the music, giving myself freely to it. My body surrenders to him, fingers skimming over his shoulder and down his back as I draw him closer. His hands trace to the center of my back in response. It's like no dance I've ever experienced before. The fluidity of motion. The heat of our bodies practically glued together.

It's intimate, much more intimate than anything I've experienced in my life. It's intimidating—scary, even—to be doing this. I want to break the eye contact we've had since the dance started, but I'm mesmerized. I can't take my hands away from him; I'm drawn in more.

Shifting as we dance, my arm goes around his shoulder, my hand now on his neck, fingers grazing his hair. My breasts are brushing against his chest, and a feeling of desire swells up inside of me. With the way our bodies are fitting together just right, it feels as though we're in bed. Under the sheets. Writhing horizontally as he sucks on my nipple and my back arches as we…

I become aware of a familiar ache down below that I haven't felt in over a year. Honestly, it's been longer, because it *felt* like longer since I've experienced a sexual high. It's not enough, though. I want more, and I want it to be Devlin to give it to me. I want him so badly. Oh, so badly. God, I want it even though I shouldn't.

Something changes in his breathing suddenly and he has that look in his eyes.

Oh no.

He abruptly yanks me from the open floor and off to the side behind a booth, where nobody can see us. He hauls my body to his and I gasp. His palms rest on my backside as he buries his face in the crook of my neck, pressing tiny kisses there.

I let out a shuddering breath. "I thought you were just going to kiss me once."

"All you have to do is tell me to stop and I'll stop," he says against my skin. He's giving me an out, a chance to leave or tell him I don't want this. I should tell him to stop; I should walk away right now. But I can't; I'm powerless to his touch. I only really ever imagined how it would feel. I never knew how much I truly craved it. How much I crave *him* at this moment.

His hands move to my waist and travel up, sliding along the bottom of my ribcage and stopping just below my breasts. I should push his roaming hands away. It's a precursor and I'm just enabling him. I grip his shirt near the waist, holding him close enough to feel his hard length press against my stomach. A yearning sound comes out of my mouth before I can prevent it. He lets out a harsh breath and starts to nip at my ears, tugging them lightly between his teeth. Moving up, he presses a kiss to my temple, then my forehead, his hand cupping my face.

"Allegra," he says softly against my cheek. My breath catches as my mind wraps around the fact that he's closing in on my lips to steal a kiss. Is it stealing a kiss when you want it? No. But…it's all too much. I'm lusting for Devlin of all people. It's a precarious road I'm heading down, the same one I stepped onto last year when I first fell for him. I want to surrender to him—surrender my body to him—and yet, I'm holding back.

I know that if I let him kiss me once, I'll be done for, unable to resist kissing him back. I won't be able to resist his touches. I want to give in, but I'm afraid of what it'll mean tomorrow. He's right—it may not be smart to have a one-night stand with a stranger, but at least with a stranger I won't have to face him again. With a stranger, there's no emotional connection. Somehow it feels like there's a chance for one with him.

He said he wouldn't kiss me right away, but he's too far gone and so am I. His face comes in closer and closer. His lips are a breath away, about to claim the kiss I promised him earlier. I can't let him because I know what will happen when he does.

Just when Devlin's lips are about to meet mine, I wrench my body away from him. He blinks rapidly, his gaze unfocused. "Allegra?"

I open my mouth, then close it, incapable of forming the words sitting there on the tip of my tongue. I mumble, "Excuse me."

He stares blankly at me, his eyes still hazy from the moment we just shared.

I run to the bar, snagging my clutch as I escape toward the elevator. Once I get to the elevator and press the button, I cross my fingers that it will open and let me in before Devlin catches up. "Come on, come on," I mumble as

I roughly press the button three more times. There's something happening to my heart and I don't like it. *Come on, brain. Why won't you keep me grounded? I don't care about the endorphins my body keeps sending you. Do your job and stop leaving the thinking to my vagina!*

When the doors open, I feel the flood of relief wash over me as I hop inside and press the button. Leaning against the back of the elevator, I bury my face in my hands and take a deep breath as I listen to the sound of the doors closing. Wait, that's not the sound of elevator doors closing.

That's when I peek through my fingers to find Devlin Pierce holding those doors open.

chapter eight

"**W**here the hell do you think you're going?" he says angrily. He steps inside and presses the button to close the doors.

My eyes widen and I gesture to the closed doors. "What the hell is your problem?"

He gapes at me. "Me? How about you? You made a promise."

"I know," I admit.

"You're afraid."

I twitch at his speculation, because I know he's right. "I'm not afraid."

"Bullshit." He pulls the emergency stop and moves in closer, almost cornering me. I suck in a breath. His nearness and the scent of him washing over me in the confined space is eliciting a reaction from my body. I want his lips on my neck again, pouring kisses like rain that slowly spread over every inch of my skin. He tilts my chin up so that my eyes can't avoid his. "You're afraid of my kiss."

"No."

"Yes, you are. Why would you be afraid of it?" He places a hand on the elevator wall behind my head. The fingers of his other hand trail along the edge of my jaw. "It couldn't be because you're worried you're going to feel something, is it?"

I shake my head, but his light touch is tantalizing. I fear I may accidentally admit how I really feel if I answer him out loud. His fingers caress the column of my neck and my breath catches in my throat. It's all I can do to keep my knees from buckling beneath me as I stand before him. My chest is moving up and down with my heavy breathing. There's a thump on the elevator floor, and I jump. Glancing down, I realize I accidentally dropped my clutch.

He leans in and whispers in my ear, "If this is how you react to me barely touching you, imagine how it would feel to have my cock buried deep inside of you."

I shiver and, closing my eyes, beg my body to resist him, but I know that resistance is futile when it comes to Devlin Pierce.

"Are you going to say anything?" he asks me. "If not, I have another way to put those pretty lips to use." He dips his head and his lips brush across mine. "Is that what you want, Allegra?"

I yell in my head, *Yes, damn it! Kiss me!* However, I say nothing.

He looks into my half-closed eyes. "Haven't you heard? Eyes are the window to your soul." He takes my upper lip between his and sucks gently. A shaky breath comes from me just before his lips close around mine. He kisses me thoroughly and deeply. At first, it feels as though he's only seducing, but then, it feels like more—like he's worshiping me. He stops, his forehead pressed to mine, and says, "I've had dreams about your lips, but none of them were close to the real thing."

His scent fills my nostrils, intoxicating me. We're not even touching, except for our foreheads, but everything feels electric. The hair on my arms is standing on end. His moves were unflinching and deliberate. Everything about that kiss has me reeling. He was right—one kiss is all a girl needs to know that Devlin Pierce means business. If I had my doubts before, I don't anymore. He's irresistible. A hidden sensation below the surface emerges, catching me off guard with its power. That's all it takes for me to cave.

My hands grip his jacket, hauling him to me as I press my lips back to his. He freezes briefly in shock, then moans at the realization that I'm giving in, his arms encircling me. His tongue teases my bottom lip, and my mouth opens to let him in. Our tongues tango in a dance as sensual as our literal one only moments ago. He explores my mouth, delving in to taste me repeatedly. My worst fear has been realized: I can't get enough of his kiss. My body is no longer held captive by the reasonings of my mind. It has taken over, collaborating with my heart to overthrow any remaining logic in my brain.

I let go of his jacket, yank his shirt out of his pants, and run my hands over his muscular abdomen. He tears his lips away from mine, his arms still holding me in place, and says, "God, I want you so badly."

"I can tell." I skim my hands down until they brush over his erection.

He releases a shuddering breath. "And what do you want?" he asks in a low voice, lips hovering over mine.

If he could feel how damp my panties have gotten since I first laid eyes on him tonight, he would know. "What do you think?" I ask as I reach around, squeezing his ass.

He growls and laughs at the same time. "Oh, what you do to me." He pushes me back against the wall and starts kissing down my neck to the swell of my cleavage. My eyes flutter closed and my fingers tangle into his hair. He groans when his trail of kisses on my skin meets the fabric of my dress. "This is in my way," he says, palming my breast. My nipple pebbles under the fabric separating his skin from my skin.

"If you even think of suggesting ripping this dress off me, I'll flog you."

"Do people still do that?" His hand travels down my

stomach to my waist, then my thighs. "I love your legs."

I feel myself flush. "They're too big."

He shakes his head as he kisses my neck. "They're perfect. Just the right size for what I want to do to you." He holds on to both of my legs, pressing his body into mine, giving me a taste of what is to come. My whole body lights up in anticipation. He's teasing me—no, *taunting* me—with every drawn out move he makes. It's almost as if he's trying to slow things down. That's not what I want, though.

I hitch up my dress and hop into his arms. He presses me back into the wall, sitting me on the railing, his hard length now at my center. I bite my lip as I feel my arousal building to greater heights. His hands feel their way up my leg and he lets out a growl. He mutters against my lips, "Thigh highs…"

I grin, loosening his tie enough to get access to his collar, then unbuttoning the top button. "Thought you'd like that."

"I don't like it."

I frown. "What?"

"I *love* it." His palms smooth over the exposed skin on my leg. It's going to be nearly impossible to take our time when he touches me like that. I shudder and, being incapable of taking my time unbuttoning each individual button on his shirt, quickly rip it open. The buttons fly, a few clinking as they hit the metal wall before landing on the carpeted floor. He stares at me, eyes wide, right before he swoops down to kiss me deeply, his tongue invading my mouth with purpose. I wrap both arms around him tightly under his shirt as he rubs against me; his erection pushes insistently against my core, causing an aching pulse of absolute want.

"Damn it," I whisper against his lips, unhooking my legs from him to stand again. I rip off his belt, then swiftly unbutton and unzip his pants. My fingers wrap around him through his boxers.

"Shit," he mumbles, cupping my cheek. "You're going to be the death of me."

"It'll be an enjoyable death," I counter as I pull his hard, thick length out. He's certainly blessed beyond any woman's fantasy. It's all I can do not to drop to my knees and take him all the way down my throat, but there is no way I can stop the overpowering urge to have him buried deep inside me. It's not as if I couldn't later tonight, right?

He sucks in a breath, his muscles tightening with restraint. "I'm going to fuck you in this elevator if you don't stop."

"I don't want to stop," I tell him as I gently bite his lip.

A low moan comes from his throat and he reaches between my legs. Pushing aside my underwear, his fingers delve into my folds. "My God, you're so wet." He begins to rub a slow circle over my nub while he presses open-mouthed kisses on my neck and jaw. I stroke up his length, causing him to lose his momentum, but he recovers a second later.

resist

The unhurried speed of his finger is killing me; I need him to go faster...I need... "Inside...I need you inside me," I say breathlessly, pulling his hand away to take off my panties.

"I can't argue with that." He lifts me back up and I guide his hard length to where it needs to go. As I line him up with my entrance, I have to admit it seems fitting that our first time would be in an elevator. In fact, it's fucking perfect.

Just as he's about to push inside me, static breaks through the air from the intercom. A scratchy voice says, "Is everyone all right in there?"

The two of us freeze in place, the head of his cock stopping its approach. Our eyes meet in an intense gaze. Neither of us speaks or moves. For a second, I almost expect him to press inside me. I mean, I want him to. With all the buildup to this moment, I can't imagine stopping now.

Despite the conflict in his eyes, Devlin clears his throat and says over his shoulder, "Yes, we're fine. Everything's fine." I loosen my grip on him and he lowers me to the floor. "Shit," he mutters under his breath.

"What?"

"I don't have a condom," he says.

It didn't even hit me until now that if we hadn't been interrupted, we would have been having unprotected sex. I'm on birth control, but still. "You don't have a condom in your pocket?"

"I expected you to want to go to my room, not stop a

damn elevator."

I shrug with a smirk. "I'm never what anyone expects."

"Amen to that."

I straighten up, adjusting my clothing while Devlin does the same. He releases the emergency stop and I reach down to get my clutch. Right when I'm about to grab my panties, Devlin snags them and shoves them in his pocket. He doesn't bother picking up the stray buttons on the floor. I'd reach down for them myself, but I can't move.

The numbers light up one by one, and second by second, we're getting closer to my floor. Despite not having a single part of our bodies touching, the sexual tension crackles in the air surrounding us. The thought of him touching me again creates a throbbing down below. I unconsciously bite my lip as I turn to Devlin.

His eyes are already on me, that intense gaze overwhelming my senses. As soon as I look at him, he reaches out and pulls me into his arms, his mouth on mine. My body tingles at the warmth of him against me, his lips hot with passion. He whispers, "Spend the night with me, Allegra."

I answer him the only way I can: "Yes."

chapter nine

We go up another couple of floors to his room. He holds my hand as we walk down the hall. Quickly swiping his key card, he pulls us both into the room. It may not be the penthouse suite, but it's certainly larger than the room I have, plus it has a kitchen. Unlike the first floor and the hallways, his room is encased in royal blue and silver accents. The curtains are drawn, but I can see a sliver of the buildings at the edge and wonder how his view compares to mine.

Before I can even take in anything more about the room, he throws his belt to the floor and presses me against the wall, his lips finding mine. When he starts mouthing from my neck to my collarbone, I breathe, "Oh, Devlin," before I can stop myself.

His hands grip my waist, and he stops what he's doing to look me in the eyes. "Did you just say my name?"

I swallow hard and nod.

A low groan comes from his throat and he presses our bodies together. "Don't stop saying my name, Allegra."

I shiver. "Only if you don't stop saying mine...Devlin." I touch a finger to his chin as I say his name.

He closes his eyes and lets out a long breath. "Maybe you shouldn't say my name."

My attempt to hide my delight in the effect I have over his body fails. I smirk and ask, "Why not?"

He moves his hands down to my thighs. "I can barely contain myself as it is. You're lucky I've been able to maintain some level of self-control around you." His arousal is still obvious, throbbing against the front of my body.

"If that's the case, you'd better fuck me here against the wall."

He growls, his palms pushing up my dress to cup my bottom, lifting me up. Wrapping my legs around him tightly, he presses me into the wall, his erection still as hard as it was in the elevator. He moves against me in the most delicious way possible. "Tell me." His breath is hot against my ear.

"Tell you what?" I ask, panting.

"Tell me you want me."

"I already told you—"

"No, you didn't. You only implied. Tell me. *Say* it."

My fingers grip his hair as I feel the pleasure building up again, but not quite reaching the edge. It's torture, but he knows what he's doing to me. He wants me to acknowledge the truth of what's happening between us. I don't even care that he's trying to expose my true feelings anymore; I can't contain the emotions swirling in my head. "Oh God, I want you, Devlin. I never stopped wanting you."

I drop out of his arms to undo his pants again. As soon as my fingers touch his erection, he lets out a hiss. "Don't," he says, pulling my hand away. "What did I just say?"

"Then, for the love of all that is holy, get a condom."

He rushes to a briefcase, and within a matter of seconds, produces and puts on a condom. He takes off his jacket quickly before he returns to me. At least I don't have to worry about taking off my panties again. As he's coming back over, I reach to unzip my dress, but he stops me. Hoisting me up and pushing me against the wall, he says, "Leave it on. I want to take it off, but I can't wait any longer to be inside you."

Gripping his broad shoulders, I let out an unsteady breath as his fingers find me, sliding through my folds. He slips a finger inside, and I gasp as he teases me at that spot I've always heard about. I've never felt anything like it. My legs wrap around his waist, holding on tightly as he brings me closer and closer, but not quite there.

He removes his finger, nudging his cock at my entrance. The head of his shaft slowly presses inside and he lowers me in one quick thrust, plunging into my depths to the hilt. I let out a choked sob, my fingers clutching at the back of his shirt, flinching at the initial pain.

His eyes bore into mine, wide with concern. "Did I hurt you?"

"No, it's just…" I let out a long breath as I close my eyes. "It's been a year since I…"

"Oh Christ, Allegra." He brings a hand to the back of my head and kisses my forehead. "You should've told me."

"Why, so you can take this slow?"

He laughs. "I swear, you're something else." He doesn't move for a moment, just kisses my lips tenderly. When he pulls away, he asks, "You ready?"

A lesser man would have kept going, not even noticing my reaction for what it was. I feel a flutter in my heart at this, but push it aside as I nod. "I'm ready."

Holding my legs firmly, he pulls out slightly then pushes back in again. It's still somewhat uncomfortable, but I feel my body accepting him. I smile as I pull him in for another kiss. He starts to move in and out of me at a slow pace, and I match his moves the best I can from this position. When he increases the speed, I start to moan against his cheek. He groans out, "Allegra, oh God…it feels so fucking good to be inside you."

His words intensify the feeling rising through my entire body. I never thought hearing a man say such things in the midst of the throes of passion would cause a physical response. It pulses in my veins, spreading a tingling feeling from my head down to my toes. "Devlin," I gasp out. "Oh, Devlin, I'm…I'm…"

That's all he has to hear and he's pumping into me furiously. I slide up the wall with every thrust, breathing out tiny cries of pleasure. It builds, rising until it reaches a glorious crescendo. The sensations roll through me, like the vibrations of cymbals crashing together at the end of an orchestra's finale. I hold onto him as the waves slowly dissipate. Coming down from my high, I can hear from the pattern of Devlin's breathing that he's about to reach his.

I grip his hair and whisper in his ear, "I want you to come, Devlin." I tug at his lobe with my teeth.

He rasps out, "Allegra, oh my God," as he releases into me with a low groan. I revel in the feel of it, almost coming again. His head falls to my shoulder. His broad chest pushes against mine as his lungs fight to return his breathing to normal. Based on how long it's taking me, I'm willing to bet it will be awhile.

I'm not quite sure how I'm supposed to feel about what just happened. I mean, I just had sex. With Devlin Pierce. Against a wall. With most of my clothes *and* the lights on. After sex with a virtual stranger, I'm supposed to feel dirty, right? Maybe experience a little bit of self-loathing? It doesn't feel like either. I don't feel the least bit dirty and I don't hate myself.

When my breath catches up to me, I say, "That was…

that was…" How do I form words after that? How do I describe how it felt—how everything felt—just now?

"The best sex you've ever had?" he asks, pressing a kiss to the spot where my neck meets my shoulder. "Because I fully agree."

"Yeah." It really was. I can't deny it.

He brings his face up to mine. "What's even better is that was only the beginning."

I blink at his words. "Beginning?" I repeat.

Furrowing his brows, he says, "Of course. You didn't expect that to be it, did you? I mean, you asked for a one-night stand. That's why I'm here. Not a quickie where I'm in and then out the door, but a full night of uninhibited passion."

"Uninhibited, huh?" My lips slowly curve up into a smile. "How so?"

He shifts, and I realize he's still inside me. "I want to have you in as many positions as possible tonight." I shudder at the thought of this, my passage clenching around him. Sucking in a breath, he warns, "Careful, or round two will be against the wall again."

I feel him start to get hard once more. *Only the beginning*, he said. My eyes widen as they look up into his. "You're insatiable."

He smirks. "Only with you."

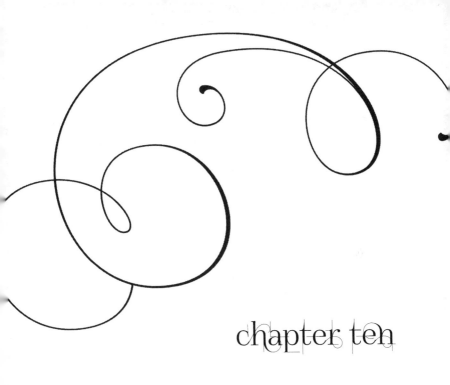

chapter ten

The thought of being the only one to fuel those desires in him thrills me like nothing else. I never thought I would elicit that kind of response in a man. "In that case," I say, "we'd better act quickly to get into this new position."

"I couldn't agree more, but first things first." He lifts me off his almost fully erect cock. Once my feet touch the floor, I realize that my heels must have fallen off somewhere in the midst of our wall sex. It takes a few seconds to regain my balance, but he steadies me with a smile. Taking both my hands in his, he pulls me with him over to the bed. He removes the condom, tossing it into the trash can. Reaching behind me, he unzips my dress and very carefully slides it down my body, allowing me to step out of it. With the dress in his hands, he glances over me, then meets my eyes.

"What?" I ask him, suddenly self-conscious and realizing my underwear is still in his pants pocket.

He shakes his head. "Nothing. It's just…you're so gorgeous."

I sense my face flushing, and my hand comes up to my cheek to cover it up. "Stop."

"Never." He lays my dress gently over a chair. "Now that your dress is taken care of, I have no desire to slow down."

"Better not." I reach out to him, unbuttoning the few buttons that didn't pop off, pulling his shirt off the rest of the way. "Sorry about your shirt. I can replace it."

"No need. This is going on my trophy wall."

"There's a wall?"

"There will be now."

I can't help but laugh as I pull his face down to mine, kissing him deeply. When he pulls my body toward his, our skin touching, I let out a moan as I think of the fact that there are still hours to go for us. I wonder how many rounds we can fit in tonight without losing too much sleep. *Who am I kidding? I'd stay up all night for this.*

His fingers play around the clasp of my bright blue lace bra, but he doesn't undo it. He just keeps slipping his fingers under. It starts to make me antsy, so I say with a groan, "Just take it off."

"You obviously put a lot of thought into what you would be wearing. I'd hate to open such a divine package without savoring the moment just a little longer."

I roll my eyes. "Seriously, just take it off."

He unclasps it with one hand, taking it off all the way. He stands back and gazes at my breasts reverently. Then his eyes flash up to mine. "Tell me what you want. What you like." His breathing is erratic as he steps closer. With no part of our bodies touching, he leans in, his face merely inches from mine. "Tell me where you want my hands, my lips, my cock."

Despite all the time I've spent discovering my own body, I still can't pinpoint exactly what gets me off. I can get there—most of the time anyway—but it's a lot of trial and error. Even when I figure something out, it doesn't work the second time. Maybe what I said earlier strikes truer than I want to believe. It's not the same. It's better with a man, but especially with Devlin Pierce. I try to ignore that fact and tell him, "Just keep doing what you're doing. I can't imagine anything better."

He kisses me deeply. "You haven't seen anything yet."

I shudder at the thought of what he could do to me. "Show me."

He growls, swooping down to suck on one of my nipples. A breathy gasp I've never heard before comes from my lips. I tangle my fingers in his hair, and struggle to remain standing as he teases my nipples with his lips and his tongue. His hands cover both of my breasts as he kisses between them.

Open-mouthed kisses make their way down my torso

until they end at the top of my mound. If he starts anything down there with that mouth of his, I swear I'm going to just collapse into a puddle on the floor and never be able to get up again.

He must be reading my mind because he stands up and lifts me onto the bed, settling me in the middle of the silky silver comforter. He removes my thigh-high stockings, his eyes never leaving mine. Once they're gone, he spreads my legs apart. He kisses up my calf, pausing at the back of my knees. As a shiver spreads through me, I can't believe the pleasures I'm feeling from such simple stimulation. Devlin knows his way around a woman's body, that's for sure.

He continues to kiss up my leg. When he gets close to the juncture between my thighs, I begin to twitch. "I love how responsive you are to my touches," he murmurs against the inside of my thigh. He places a palm between my legs and I suck in a breath. "Do you feel sore at all?"

I shake my head as I look down at him. "No. It's fine now actually. It was just the initial move that…well…"

"I know." He kisses my inner thigh again gently. "If it were up to me, I'd make sure you were never self-sufficient again."

The familiar tingling increases at the thought, and my body involuntarily shifts closer to him.

He smirks. "Tempting, isn't it?"

"I'm not dignifying that with a response."

"Why can't you just admit it?"

Lots of reasons, I think. "Why are you so desperate to hear it if you already know?"

"Inquiring minds...I'm glad you're feeling better here."

"Why?"

"Because I want to see what kind of response I'll get from you when I do this." He descends on me in a flash, his mouth sucking on my clit.

I let out a cry as my back arches. My hands hold onto his head as he licks up and down, his tongue laving at me. Several nonsensical words manage to break through between my tiny cries. Two fingers slip in and out of me as he swirls his tongue over my sensitive nub. He's drawing out more pleasure than I ever imagined possible between the two moves, so much so that when I come, my whole body shakes. I whisper his name on repeat until it ends.

When I open my eyes, I find him standing before me at the foot of the bed, fully naked. He's about to climb back onto the bed when I say, "Wait."

He stops. "What?"

"Just...let me look at you." My eyes rake over his body, drowning in how perfect it is. Well, it's not *that* perfect, but to me it is. His biceps, his chest, his abs, and the marvelous cock that's standing at attention because of me. He's better than I desire; he's *everything* I desire. I don't know what I did to deserve this—a man who is obviously deeply interested in taking care of me tonight—but I'm thankful for whatever it was. Maybe this is just for the night, but my God, what a night of glory this is already.

His eyebrows go up, curious about my sudden interest in his body. With a tilt of his head, he says, "Permission to come aboard?"

"That's what she said."

He shakes his head. "Only you." He climbs up between my still-open legs, a condom package in his hand.

I snatch it from him and rip it open. "Allow me." I place the condom on the tip of his erection and glide it down. I press a kiss to the tip before lying back on the bed.

He stares at me with a wicked gleam in his eye. "That was one of the sexiest things I've ever seen in my entire life."

"Really?"

"Absolutely." His lips fuse to mine, purposely allowing his thick member to slide through my folds, but not inside me. I buck beneath him, unable to restrain myself. Damn him for teasing me. In that case, nobody can hold me responsible for my actions.

Quickly, I maneuver my legs and flip us so that I'm on top. I wrap my hands around his cock, placing him at my entrance and sinking down on him until he's fully sheathed inside of me. He moans deep enough that I feel the vibration where we're connected. "My God," he mutters, his hand coming to my face to draw me down for a kiss. "You're full of surprises."

I move against him slowly. "You said as many positions as possible, so…"

"You made an excellent choice."

I sit back up, his hands on my hips. I find a rhythm and he matches my moves upward. My head falls back, arousal rippling through me every time he hits me deep. Guttural sounds emerge from my throat. "So good," I say, unable to think of anything else to verbalize the feeling.

"So very good," he says in agreement. His fingers graze up my body until they land on my breasts, massaging them with his hands.

God, that feels amazing. "Keep doing that." *Never stop doing that*, I think.

"You like it?"

"I *love* your hands on me," I admit.

"I'll remember that." He continues to stroke me, sliding his hands down around my stomach and my waist and my back, then back up to my breasts again. My body tingles all over with every new sensation that comes from each place his hand touches. Looking down at him, my hands caress over his stomach to his chest, then over his arms. His eyes lock onto mine and he says, "I love your hands on me, too." His voice is laden with hunger. He wants more, and so do I.

"Good." I start to move faster against him, keeping my hands on his chest for stability, allowing the pleasure to swell from his thick member inside. My eyes are on his, absolutely captivated by the dark pools they have become. The intensity transforms into something overwhelming, and I'm on the verge of my orgasm. All Devlin has to do is rub circles over my nipples with his fingers, and I lose it. I clench around him as I come, drawing his release within seconds of mine. He shudders beneath me, and I savor how extraordinary it feels to be the one to experience it.

My hands drift up to his shoulders and curl around them as I exhale. He draws me down onto him and we lay there for a moment in each other's arms, just breathing. For some reason, I can't imagine a better feeling—a better moment—than this.

chapter eleven

I sit back up and carefully lift myself off him, collapsing on my back right next to him. "No offense," I tell him, "but I hope you don't recover as quickly as you did the last time."

"Why not?"

"I need to catch my breath."

He laughs. "So do I." We lie side by side, our breathing gradually returning to normal. After a minute, he sits up and says, "I think I need to hydrate, too. Would you like a glass of water?"

"Yes, please."

He presses a quick kiss to my forehead before rolling off the bed to his feet. I sit up on my elbows to watch him as he walks to the kitchen. His bare-naked ass is even better than the view I had with his pants on earlier tonight. I bite my lip to keep from smiling, but it's no use. He calls from the kitchen, "Enjoying the view?"

"Very much so, yes."

His laugh echoes through the hotel room. "Good to know."

He returns, handing me the glass of water, and I thank him as I sit up to drink it. Strangely, I don't feel as naked as I am—it feels natural. Normal. I'm generally not this open with men, but in front of Devlin my nudity isn't even stirring up the nerves it usually does.

Breaking the silence, he says, "So…a year?"

I cringe as I recall my admission from earlier. "Yes."

"Please tell me it's wasn't because of what happened with me last year."

I shake my head, cradling the glass between both of my hands. "It wasn't. Technically, it's been a year and two months. Last somewhat boyfriend."

"Somewhat?"

"It's hard for me to have a serious relationship. More like it was hard for my somewhat boyfriend to." I shrug it off, not wanting the memories to resurface. They're the ones that led me to where I am and I refuse to let them take me down again. I push them back into the vault and close the door. "It's just too bad."

"What is?"

"That we missed out on this a year ago."

"I think it's better."

I turn to him, head tilted. "How so?"

He gives me a smirk. "Pent up sexual frustration can only culminate in a night like tonight."

"I can't argue with that." I glance over at the window and sigh at the curtain covering the city. When I left the dinner, it was a little after eight. At this point it has to be well past ten, most likely close to eleven. I wish it were summer so I could watch the sun descending into the horizon. Why does the annual company dinner happen in February? I sigh again.

"What?"

I dangle my legs off the bed. "I want to look out your window."

"Go ahead."

I turn back to him. "I'm not standing naked in front of a window in New York City for the world to see."

"Nobody would see you. Except me." He smirks.

"Of course." Still, I hesitate. I can have sex with someone I barely know and feel comfortable sitting around naked, yet I'm paranoid of a peeping tom ogling at my stuff if I open the curtains.

"What if I turn the lights off?" He gets up and dims the lights until all I can see are the lights outside through the glass. I place my glass on the nightstand as I stand up and cross the room to the window. I tug at the curtains, pulling them to the side to reveal the city. The familiar delight flickers upon first sight. His view is only slightly different from mine, yet it feels like it's brand new. I tilt my head, trying to count the lights that are still on in the buildings surrounding us, but there are as many windows lit up as there are stars in the sky. "I don't think I could ever get over the beauty of it."

"You love the city?" he asks me from the bed.

"I adore it."

"Then why don't you move here?"

"Lots of reasons…"

"Such as?"

"First off, it's far too expensive. I don't know anyone who would be willing to move here with me, and I sure as hell wouldn't move here alone. That would be too ridiculous." I shake my head. "Not only that, but I'm not a city girl. It's perfect for a vacation or a weekend, but I would miss being near my family and my childhood home too much."

"Where do they live?"

"About three hours from Cleveland, in the country." I hold out my forefinger to trace the buildings and the sky. "I may like the glitter of the Big Apple, but I like the quiet outside the city more. Makes me nostalgic." A chill comes over me as I stand there in my birthday suit, goose bumps beginning to pop up over my arms. I cross my arms over my chest as I continue to stare at the skyline.

"In that case, maybe Jack could let you go on business trips here throughout the year." Devlin comes over, wrapping his arms around me from behind. "That way you can have the best of both worlds."

I relax into the warmth of his embrace, wondering for a fleeting moment if he noticed that I'm cold or if he just wanted to hold me. "Yeah. That would be nice. How about you?"

"New York is a beautiful city, and I might consider living here for a spell, but not forever." He nuzzles his nose into my disheveled hair. When I laugh, he asks, "What?"

"I probably look like a mess." I reach a hand back to touch his cheek as he continues the nuzzling.

"You look beautiful."

"Stop it."

"No. I never lie about beauty." His hands caress my stomach and hips. "What's next?"

Based on his hard length pressing against my backside, I'm guessing round three is next. I settle my arms over his. "Hmm… I don't know." I tilt my head back to press a kiss to his lips. "What do you have in mind?"

He glances toward the window. "Right here."

I spin around to face him head on, my eyes wide. "Against the window?" Where everyone could see my skin pressing against the glass? I don't think I'm ready for the world to catch a glimpse of my pressed ham.

He laughs. "Not against—in front of. Don't be so afraid." He tucks a hair behind my ear. "Nobody will see us. And so what if they do? They don't know us. We're in

New York. We're tourists, strangers…people are completely oblivious to what we're doing."

"I don't know…" I shift from one foot to the other.

Devlin touches a finger to his lips. "What will it take to convince you? Ah, I know." He spins me back around, my back against his front. Bending me forward with one arm around my middle, he says, "How about I give you a glimpse of what I have in mind? Place your hands on the sill."

I do what he asks as he stands up, spreading my legs just enough to slip a finger inside. My fingers grip tighter to brace myself, and I close my eyes at the feel of one mere finger pressing against the spot. It doesn't take long before I'm feeling that pleasure climbing high. "How are you so good at this?" I accidentally say out loud.

He laughs, slowing the pace and then removing his finger entirely. He leans down, arm back around me, and whispers in my ear, "Don't sound so surprised. I'm a man of *many* talents."

"Is giving a girl blue balls one of them?" I ask, squirming to rub against his erection.

His breath comes out in a hiss. "Just a second. Don't move." He pulls away and the loss of him causes a dull ache in my heart even though I know he's coming back. I hear the sound of the condom wrapper, and within seconds he's back against me. In one swift move, he pushes deep inside me. I let out a cry of surprise. He leans forward, an arm coming around to caress my nipples. "I was planning on taking my time," he whispers against my skin, kisses feathering my back and shoulder.

"It's okay, I didn't need any more foreplay. I like it." He starts to pump into me and my eyes flutter closed. "Oh, I like it a lot."

His lips twitch into a smile against my skin. "Me too, Allegra. Me too."

"Oh…uhn…ohhhh…"

"I love the sounds you make when my cock is inside you," Devlin says in a low voice as he swirls a finger over my clit.

"Oh God." My fingers dig into the sill. The waves begin to crest with every thrust. The sound of our skin slapping together echoes throughout the room, and somehow that raises the level of desire in me. "Devlin," I gasp. "Harder, Devlin."

With a throaty growl in his chest, he stands, gripping my thighs with both hands. He pistons into me, driving me to the brink and I come apart beneath him with a low moan and a shudder. I'm barely able to hang on, feeling as though I could just collapse to the floor before he's done. I expect him to let go soon, but he keeps hanging on. He wraps his arm around me again, his other hand sliding between my legs. "Come with me, Allegra," he murmurs in my ear as he rubs circles over my clit. I fall apart again, thankful that he's holding on to me. When I scream out his name, he's unable to hold back any longer. He yells, "Fuck!" right before he releases inside me.

I don't know how he manages to, but he remains standing. I can't believe how exhausted I already am, and it's barely after midnight. How is he able to keep it together so easily? The man has stamina like nobody's business. Just when he's about to take his hands off me, I say, "Don't let go. I don't think I can stand on my own power."

His chuckle reverberates through me. "Don't worry, I've got you." He slowly pulls out of me, and then quickly lifts me into his arms. I wrap my arms around his shoulders without hesitation and rest my face against his cheek. This feels…safe. I feel safe in his arms. I shouldn't, I know I shouldn't. Yet, I do.

He carries me across the room and into the bathroom. He sets me down on my feet. "Hold on to the sink for a second."

"What are you doing?"

"What do you think?" he asks, turning the shower knobs until a blast of water comes raining down. "We're taking a shower."

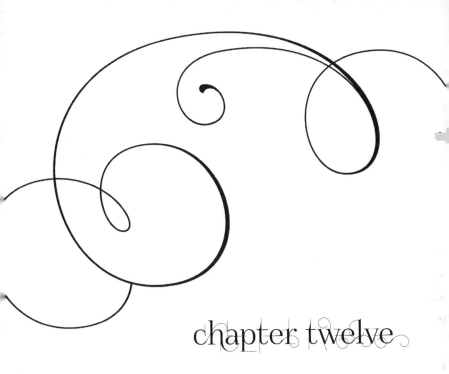

chapter twelve

"We're what?" I ask him, incredulous.

He takes my hands and pulls me into the shower with him. "I think it's necessary."

I back into the hot spray and savor how great it feels. "Are you saying I smell?"

"A little bit." I smack his arm, laughing despite myself, while he grins. He leans down and says, "Trust me, this has nothing to do with smelling."

"Then what is it for?"

He reaches for the shampoo. "We're taking a break to get our strength back." Squirting a bit into his hand, he begins to lather it into my hair.

I close my eyes as he massages the shampoo in. "Does it have to be in the shower?"

"Yes."

"Do we have to be naked?"

"Of course." He kisses my nose and gently leans my head back to wash out the shampoo. After a moment, he says, "I have to know, have you always had a way with words?"

I chuckle. "Yeah, but more so in recent years." I pick up the shampoo bottle and proceed to wash his hair, then switch spots so he stands under the water. "My dad encouraged it, while my stepmom calls my manner of speaking unbecoming of a lady."

He lets out a chuckle. "What would your mom say?"

I stop running my fingers through his hair as a twinge of pain rings through my heart. "I wish I knew. She died when I was a toddler."

He frowns, taking my hand in his and pressing his lips to my fingers. "I'm sorry, Allegra."

Usually the way people react to finding that out irritates me because it feels almost like an automatic reaction to say that you're sorry for somebody's loss. But with him, it's different. It's sincere, but it doesn't feel like pity. His kindness undoes me in that moment. It causes me to get on my tiptoes, the front of our bodies touching, and press my lips to his. He returns the kiss, slowly and gently.

We take turns washing each other. At one point, he slides his soapy hands down my legs. Upon standing up, he places kisses around my waist. Once we're completely clean he grabs a towel, drying off my arms and legs before wrapping it around me. As we stand here drying off, it feels as though something has changed between us, but I can't quite put my finger on it. When he looks at me fondly, it hits me:

He has rendered me breathless.

Damn it all. This isn't supposed to happen. This is just a distraction—an exquisite one, of course—but nothing more. That's all we want. Yet, a strange sensation is overcoming me and I desire more. Tonight is all that is going to happen, though. Just one night. That's why it's called a one-night stand, after all.

Ignore those feelings, Allegra. He made it clear where he stands. I'm looking for something he's not offering, and that's okay. It's okay to let myself go just this once. There's a voice in my head screaming to leave. Yet I can't turn away, can't walk away until this moment finishes. I'm going to live in it, breathe it in.

I gaze back up into those gorgeous eyes. I unravel the towel from my body and let it fall to the floor. In a soft voice, I say, "I want to feel your hands all over me."

He inhales deeply and slides his fingers across my collarbone. I shudder. "As you wish." He takes my hand in his and presses a kiss to the top of it. Then, cradling the back of my neck with the other hand, his lips sweep across mine and his mouth captures my sigh. He tastes like honey and heaven. I could kiss him for hours. Devlin Pierce can kiss better than anybody else.

I walk backwards out of the bathroom, our lips never separating. He guides us back to the bed. The back of my legs hit the edge of the bed and we stand here, just kissing. It's tender for a minute, but in the next our tongues are dueling for control. I pull away from his lips, scanning his eyes to solve the puzzle that he is. The fondness remains, as does the puzzle. But I let the questions fade away and give myself to the moment.

I'm about to climb onto the bed when he stops me. His hands cup my cheeks and he presses a kiss to my forehead, trailing down to my lips again. All the while his hands slide down my neck, shoulders, arms…then my waist up to my breasts, lingering there for a moment before going to my stomach, hips, legs…

My skin is lighting up like a flame on every spot he caresses, and everywhere his touch was a second ago, there's a tingle that whispers in its wake. A thrill shoots throughout my body and I ache to feel more of him on my skin. I reach out to his chest with my palms, breathing out a sigh.

His kisses move to my ear and he whispers, "Touch me. More. All over."

I smooth my hands over his chest, rubbing my thumbs over his nipples. He chuckles against my skin, and I join him. "You asked for it."

"I did." He shivers when I press my lips to each of them lightly. I touch the hard muscles of his stomach and wind my arms around to his back. My hands caress every inch as

resist

I bring our bodies together, my breasts settling just below his smooth chest. My ear is right against his heart and I can hear it race. He sucks in a breath and I notice that he lost his towel somewhere along the line as his hard length presses into me. "You're making this hard."

"I know. Wait, making what hard?"

He laughs. "I'm determined to take it slow this time around."

"How slow?"

He steps back out of my arms and touches a finger to my lips. I press them together, biting back a smile. I hop onto the bed, slowly crawling up the silky cover until I reach the pillows. He watches me intently, letting out an appreciative sigh along with a smile. I motion with my fingers for him to come closer, and he obliges with a slow crawl up the bed and over my body. He gradually lowers himself on me. It doesn't take long for our lips to meet and our bodies to tangle together.

It has never been like this before—the leisurely pace and the attentiveness. I only ever expect it to be over all too soon with my lovers, as has been the case in the past. With Devlin, it's different, and wonderfully so.

He kisses down my throat, across my neck and collarbone. His hand deftly slips between my legs, and I willingly open up to him. His fingers are on me down there and I twitch with every touch and stroke. I'm coming apart already and he's not even inside me, not even his fingers. He rolls his thumb over my clit in lazy circles. My breath comes out in gasps. "I want you inside me," I manage to say.

"I want to be inside you. Just be patient, princess." If he were anyone else, I might be annoyed with the term of endearment. But coming from his lips, I can't imagine anything more lovely. He holds me closer to him, my face in the crook of his neck. A few deliberate strokes in just the right manner and I fall apart, gasping in his arms.

Momentarily satiated and attempting to steady my heartbeat, I feel his body leave mine. My eyes shoot open when I realize this, but somehow he's already above me again, and I smile. He smiles back as he settles between my legs. His hand gently brushes my hair away from my face and cups my cheek. I reach up for his face, reveling in the stubble that has appeared since I first laid eyes on him tonight. It's insanely sexy in every way. I pull him down to bring our lips back together. While we kiss, he slowly sinks into me, filling me completely and drawing out a long sigh from my lips.

He moans as he begins to rock into me. With his forehead pressed to mine, he says in a husky voice, "I love being inside of you."

Those words nearly push me over the edge again. "I love it when you're inside me." The edges of his lips curl up slightly, clearly appreciative of my response.

I wrap my legs around his back and we move together at a slow pace. Our eyes are open and on each other. I

resist

recall what he talked about earlier when it came to trust.
Eye contact. I never thought about how important it is until just now. The way he gazes at me—his eyes completely
fixed on mine—can only point to one thing. It's not lust. It's
something I'm not expecting, something that can't be true.
Because of this, there's a tingling climbing up my spine and
spreading throughout my body that I'm unable to control.
It builds with each and every thrust, every time he's buried deep, the friction of every move. The sensations roar
through me at the speed of a train.

Holding himself up with just one arm, he slides his
hand along my body, over almost every inch he can possibly
touch. I unconsciously close my eyes, giving myself to the
pleasure of his palm stroking across my skin. He gradually
increases his speed, and then his hand is back on my cheek.
His lips are near my ear, and they whisper, "Allegra, open
your eyes." They flutter open and he pulls back to look into
them. "That's my girl," he murmurs, rocking into me deeper
than he has before.

Nothing could have prepared me for the shockwaves
that follow that move. I cry out, my hands gripping his
shoulders, eyes never leaving his. As he watches me come
undone beneath him, I can see something erupt in his eyes.
That same look I saw only moments ago. His eyes hold mine
in the final seconds, almost reverent. When he comes, I find
that I'm breathless again, causing me to come once more.

He lowers himself, his cheek against mine. We cling to

each other for a moment. It's almost as if neither one of us wants to move, even though we know we have to eventually. Yet, right now, we don't seem to care.

chapter thirteen

I close my eyes, memorizing the way it feels to have our bodies connected. Tomorrow morning, this will all be gone. Our moment is fleeting and I need to clutch on to the memory before it floats away. Because it inevitably will.

Devlin raises himself up and touches my cheek, kissing my lips lightly. "I'll be right back." He pulls out of me carefully and heads to the bathroom. While I'm slightly wired, I'm more exhausted than anything. I know I should go to my room, but I can hardly move. Taking a deep breath, I lift myself up and slip underneath the covers onto the five-hundred-thread count sheets.

A few minutes later, he returns, turning off the light and crawling under the covers next to me. In one fluid motion, his arms wrap around me and he brings me closer, resting my breasts against his chest. I hook my leg over his leg and snuggle up to him. He kisses my forehead and sighs.

"What?" I ask him.

"I'm so tired."

"We can sleep."

"I promised all night."

"You promised nothing…except the positions."

"There were so many we didn't have the chance to get to," he murmurs in an insanely sexy voice.

My skin tingles at the thought of other positions. How it would feel… "I think four times over the span of a few hours is pretty amazing."

"Four and a half," he corrects.

"Half?"

"The elevator half counts."

I laugh. "I suppose it does. Okay, the four *and a half* times were pretty amazing."

"They were. Pretty fucking amazing."

I trace my fingers over his chest absently as his fingers caress my back. I lift up my head and press a kiss to his lips. "Thank you."

"For what?"

"Tonight."

"No need to thank me. It was my pleasure."

"I don't want you to think that I don't appreciate it, because—"

"Allegra," he interrupts, touching his forefinger to my

lips. "Trust me, you don't need to say anything. I would have been willing with or without your mission."

He skims his fingertips along the edge of my jaw, his eyes following where his fingers trace. There's a tingling in my chest that seems to flutter and bounce off my ribcage. The desire seeps into my skin wherever he touches. His eyes flicker to mine suddenly. The way he watches me so lovingly, a wonderful feeling emerges from within. I haven't felt this way since…since…

Since right before I first locked that vault.

Damn it. *Damn it, damn it, damn it!* I thought I could distance myself enough from one night and come out indifferent and renewed. Instead, I'm longing to hang on and never let go. How could I have allowed myself to be ignorant of the way he stirs feelings of forever in me? There's an inconsistency in him. His saccharine words and the longing in his eyes are a contradiction that could break me.

My chest tightens. I don't know what to do. Part of me wants to stay, spend the night, and wake up next to this wonderful man. The other part of me wants to get the hell out of here before any damage can be done. I'm dangerously close to crossing a line that I can't uncross without consequences. Emotional consequences.

"Allegra?" His voice breaks me out of my trance.

I meet his curious eyes. "Yes?"

"Did I lose you there for a second?"

"It's the exhaustion, I think." I half smile to hide the

truth.

His hand brushes my hair back. "It's okay. We can sleep. We should sleep."

"Okay," I say with a nod. I lean in and press my lips to his in a chaste kiss. "Goodnight."

He laughs lightly. "That's all you've got?" Before I can respond, he slides his fingers into my hair and draws me to him. Then his lips touch mine, gentle and tender. Our lips move together harmoniously, as if they are lost in a song only they can sing.

When the kiss breaks, I feel like I ran a marathon. We barely kissed—there wasn't even any tongue. Yet, he took my breath away. Now that's talent.

He presses his lips to my forehead, then whispers, "Goodnight, Allegra."

I lay my head back on his chest. "Goodnight, Devlin."

I relax into the warmth of his body, willing sleep to rest upon my head, but it won't. As the seconds turn into minutes, I follow his steady breathing until it fades and he's sleeping. I watch his chest move slowly up and down, my hand drawing circles, hoping that sleep will be near for me, too. But it's to no avail.

After giving full control over to my body in the elevator, my brain has decided to come out and play, and is now on overdrive. What am I doing? How did I get to this place? This is what I wanted: a night of passion. I don't regret this, not for a second. Not simply due to how spectacular it felt—

which was pretty damn spectacular—but because I needed to know. It has been a question in my subconscious since last year. I could speculate for hours on end about why I shouldn't have, but I believe that if I didn't I would have regretted *that* instead. There's more frustration in not doing something than doing it in the end.

Still, there are feelings coming over me, strange ones. I wish I could put a finger on them—on the flutter in my heart and stomach. It's almost like both euphoria and sadness. I don't like it one bit because it scares me. It reminds me of the past, and I'm not a fan of the past so much.

Stupid brain. How *dare* you start working now? Why did you allow my body to do things that went straight to my heart? They're all about action and emotion; they can't think like you can. I squeeze my eyes shut. Maybe this was a bad idea after all. Who knew a one-night stand could fuck with your head so much?

I untangle myself from his embrace, mindful of the fact that the last thing I need right now is him waking up. I sit on the bed next to him and just look at him. Take in his features, his luscious lips and that sexy stubble. I could easily be with him; he proved to me that we could have a really good time. Part of me wants to stay, really I do, but I already know it would be a glorious mistake. It would be fun at first, like a honeymoon, but it would crash and burn in no time. Sexual chemistry can only go so far in a relationship. I shake my head. Why does my mind keep returning to possibilities that could never happen?

What are we going to say to each other tomorrow? It just feels like it's going to be all sorts of holy awkward and I don't want to live through that. Maybe I don't have to. I need to get out of here before I have an emotional breakdown on the floor in the fetal position.

Slipping out from under the covers, I place my feet on the floor quietly. I glance over to make sure I haven't stirred him from his slumber. He's still fast asleep. I breathe a sigh of relief. Tiptoeing across the plush carpet, I gather up my clothes and dress myself. All I can find is my dress, bra, and stockings. Where did my underwear—

Oh. *Right*… Damn it. Where are Devlin's pants? I bite my lips and scan the floor. Just when I find them, he stirs and turns to his side, facing me. I freeze, holding my breath. Please don't wake up. After a minute with no movement on his part, I decide my best bet is to escape while I can, panties or no panties. It wouldn't be the first time I've gone commando. Plus, it's not like I can't make a trip back to Victoria's Secret when I get back home.

I creep across the floor, picking up my clutch and heels. I don't bother to put on my heels. With one final glance back to Devlin, I sneak out the door. On the way back to my room, I have a realization. I could go to sleep in my hotel bed, wake up in the morning, and head back to the airport with Jack tomorrow afternoon. But if I do that, Devlin will still be at the hotel and I may run into him. Scratch that, I *will* run into him. He and Jack will want to say goodbye. What's worse than walking out on a one-night stand? Walking out on a one-night stand and running into said one-night stand the next morning.

So what do I do? The only thing that makes sense. Pack all my bags and check out of the hotel.

As I stand on the curb waving my hand for the closest taxi, I feel a pang of unease in my chest, like I *am* making a mistake, like I *should* stay. But I can't. I do what I can to keep my feelings in check. I escape. I run. Overly dramatic much? Perhaps. But it's the only way I've been able to survive since closing the vault.

I take one last look at the hotel and the buildings surrounding it and let out a sigh. "Goodbye, New York," I whisper. "Hello, next chapter."

the end

acknowledgements

Enormous thank yous…To Marie for the cover, beta reading, and formatting. To Stephanie for editing. To Rachael and Susan for beta reading. To R.W. for listening to me read Resist out loud and essentially being my alpha reader, er, listener. To everyone else who provided notes and ARC reviews on Goodreads. A special mention goes to the lovely Heather who provided the first review.

Hugs all around for my family, friends, fans, and supporters for all you do and say to brighten my day and cheer me on. A thank you in advance for everyone reading this book or any of my stories anytime. You give me the encouragement to keep writing and I'm blessed to be able to have you around.

I love you all!

XOXO,

Lilly Avalon

about the author

Lilly Avalon writes new adult and erotic romances. She's in her twenties and lives in a cute little apartment in a small city. She loves reading romantic stories as much as she loves writing them. Her favorite things include dancing, watching scandalous television dramas, and autumn. Lilly Avalon is a pseudonym.

Excerpt from

HERE
All Along

Chapter One

"I need a drink. Now."

After tossing—fine, *throwing*—my purse and keys on the couch, I march straight into the kitchen. No more delays; it's time to forget tonight. It's been yet another night like all the other first dates that never meet a second one. When you begin to lose count, that's when it's *really* time for a drink.

Adrian stands there, leaning against the counter in an unbuttoned dress shirt and dark wash jeans. He glances at me as I walk in. "How was your date?" he asks, taking a swig of his scotch.

I brush past him on my mission, opening the cupboard and moving a couple bottles around. I reiterate, "I need alcohol."

Out of the corner of my eye, I catch him hiding a smile before he says, "That bad?"

My face twitches as I ignore his line of questioning. It is more like a statement he wants me to clarify, even though he already knows the answer. Instead, I ask, "I have vodka left, don't I?" I stand on my tiptoes in hopes of spotting something in the very back. Nothing.

He waltzes over and looks with me, his chin almost touching my shoulder. "I think you polished that one off after last week's date." His voice is low right next to my ear, very nearly causing a shiver.

I let out a groan of exasperation as I recall that last drop of vodka. "Damn it!" It was the flavored kind, too. Adrian remembers everything. If he remembers the vodka, he probably remembers when I finished off the Kahlua the week before. It's becoming a trend—a very bad one.

Shutting the cupboard door, I spin around to face him, giving him a once-over for the first time since I got home. The fact that his five o'clock shadow beginning to show up more or less demonstrates his effort today. Tilting my head to the side, I ask, "What's up with this?" as I touch his jaw line with my index finger. "And this?" I pinch the collar on his shirt. "Actually, I'm more surprised you still have your clothes on."

"It's not like I walk around naked all the time."

"*Almost* naked."

"Hey," he says, pointing at me sternly. "It was just that one time."

I bite my lip recalling that day I caught him walking down the hallway in just his boxers. I'd freaked out at first, but it was a nice sight now that I think about it. Very nice. "Maybe it was."

"I'm your roommate, not your boyfriend." He touches a finger to my chin. "I make sure I'm decent in front of you until you say otherwise." His smile morphs into a smirk.

Made in the USA
Middletown, DE
07 August 2016